For my father, Barry Hector Baker (1927–1999) and my father-in-law,
Ronald Joseph Alfred Smith (1929–2009)

First U.S. edition 2013

Library of Congress Catalog Card Number 2012942376
ISBN 978-0-7636-6370-4

TLF 17 16 15 14 13 12
10 9 8 7 6 5 4 3 2 1

Printed in Dongguan, Guangdong, China

This book was typeset in Godlike-Regular and Braganza ITC Light.
The illustrations were created digitally.

Designed by Mike Jolley
Edited by Libby Hamilton

TEMPLAR BOOKS

an imprint of Candlewick Press
99 Dover Street
Somerville, Massachusetts 02144
www.candlewick.com

Acknowledgments

I would like to thank my wife, Linda, for her inspiration, and
sheer gorgeousness and for rescuing some key spreads
by the careful application of her artistic eye. Also my
children—Albie, Flossie, and Lillie—whose energy and
enthusiasm remains undiminished despite my pleas for quiet
and who will, I'm sure, fly to and walk upon those distant
peaks that I only glimpse through the mist.
    I also want to thank the wonderful people at Templar for
helping me to achieve my dream. Their bold approach to
publishing has made them a veritable force of nature!
I particularly want to thank Mike Jolley, who makes it all look
so good with his boundless patience and creativity.
    And also to the hound Rodney Seal for his consummate
professionalism in front of the camera and his truly magnificent
ears! And to his owners—Jeremy, Ashley, Anna, and Lizzie—
thank you for giving him the time off from whatever it is that
he normally does! Without him, this book would definitely
have fewer dogs in it.

FArTHER

Grahame Baker-Smith

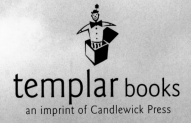

templar books
an imprint of Candlewick Press

POPPIES LINED THE PATH TO MY FATHER'S HOUSE.
IT WAS MADE OF STONE AND SLATE
AND FASTENED DEEP INTO THE CLIFF.
IT WAS SAFE AND ROOTED IN THE ROCK.
BUT INSIDE, MY FATHER DREAMED
OF AIR
AND
FLIGHT.

DAY AND NIGHT, HE SEWED AND STITCHED
AND SAWED AND HAMMERED
AND TRIMMED THE FEATHERS
OF A THOUSAND
HOPEFUL
WINGS.

BUT SOMETIMES THERE WAS SILENCE.

MY FATHER WOULD APPEAR AND STARE AT THE OCEAN
WITH TIRED, DISTANT EYES.

I WOULD SIT
ON HIS LAP UNTIL
HE REMEMBERED ME.

THEN, LIKE A GREAT WIND,
HE WOULD SCOOP ME UP
AND RUN OUTSIDE . . .

ALONG THE OLD CLIFF PATHS . . .   OVER THE ROCKS . . .

ONTO THE BEACH.

WE WOULD FISH AND SWIM AND PLAY CRICKET.
HE WOULD TEACH ME THE NAMES OF ALL THE BIRDS.

WE WOULD BE TOGETHER . . .
UNTIL THE DREAM
OF FLYING
RETURNED.

SUCH A BUSY,
BOSSY DREAM
THAT WOULD NOT LEAVE HIM ALONE
OR GIVE HIM TIME TO PLAY OR SLEEP
OR THINK OF OTHER THINGS.

OR EVEN HAVE THE GRACE TO COME TRUE.
FOR MY FATHER, AFTER ALL, NEVER FLEW.
THOUGH HE MADE SO MANY BEAUTIFUL THINGS

AND SO MANY LOVELY WINGS . . .

NOTHING HE DID COULD CLAIM THE SKY.

BUT THEN ANOTHER CALL CLAIMED HIM.

I WILL ALWAYS REMEMBER THE DAY HE LEFT —
THE CLOTHES THEY GAVE HIM, KHAKI AGAINST
THE SCARLET POPPIES.

MANY YEARS PASSED,

AND MY FATHER'S DREAM

WAITED UNTIL I WAS ALMOST GROWN.

AND THEN ONE DAY
IT SPOKE TO ME.

I TOOK UP
THE OLD WINGS,
MADE A FEW SIMPLE ADJUSTMENTS . . .

AND FLEW.

IN THE VAST BLUE SKY, I FELT MY FATHER WITH ME.

I SOON BECAME A COMMON AND EVERYDAY SIGHT AROUND THESE PARTS,

MAKING MYSELF USEFUL AND HELPING WHEREVER I COULD.

AND NOW I HAVE MY OWN SON.

WHAT WILL HE DO,
I WONDER,
IF MY FATHER'S DREAM
SHOULD VISIT HIM?